The Debt

By

Hastings Lewis

The Debt

ISBN:

ISBN-13:

Iris,

This book is dedicated to you, my constant support and love. It's written with the hope of freeing us from the burdens of debt and forging a brighter future together. Thank you for standing by me, for believing in us, and for dreaming of a better tomorrow.

With all my love,

Hastings

CHAPTER ONE

A Thin Line

The morning sun peeked timidly through the worn curtains of Carol's small kitchen, casting long shadows across the cluttered countertops strewn with yesterday's dishes and unpaid bills. The smell of strong coffee filled the air, a stark contrast to the silence of the early hour. Carol, with her hair pulled back in a hurried ponytail, maneuvered around a pair of small, sleepy-eyed children seated at the table. Her movements were swift and practiced as she prepared breakfast—a cheap box of cereal and half a gallon of milk nearing its expiration.

"Mommy, my toast is cold," complained Emily, the younger of the two, her voice a whiny contrast to the quiet determination on Carol's face.

"Just eat it up, honey. We're running late," Carol replied, her voice gentle yet edged with fatigue. She

3

glanced at the clock, its ticking a relentless reminder of the morning's fleeting peace.

As the children ate, Carol's gaze drifted to the stack of envelopes by the microwave. The red stamps screamed 'Past Due' in a bureaucratic menace that seemed to shrink the room further. She sifted through them, her fingers pausing on an electric bill that threatened disconnection. Each envelope felt heavier than the last, a tangible manifestation of the weight she carried daily.

The rattle of the old, battered car pulling up outside broke her reverie. She peered through the window to see Mike stepping out, his figure imposing against the backdrop of her fragile peace. Carol's heart sank; she knew why he was there.

Mike knocked softly, a courtesy at odds with the nature of his visit. Opening the door, Carol forced a smile, "Morning, Mike."

"Morning, Carol. Sorry to start your day like this." His voice carried a warmth that didn't quite reach his eyes. "I need to talk about the rent."

Inside, they sat at the kitchen table, an island in the chaos of Carol's life. Mike pulled out his papers, the numbers on them cold and impersonal. "You're two months behind, Carol. I need something today, even if it's not the full amount."

Carol's hands trembled slightly as she clasped them together. "Mike, I've been picking up extra shifts at the diner, and I'm trying to get something stable in the evenings, but it's just... it's been hard with the kids and everything."

Her voice was a mix of desperation and quiet dignity. Mike looked around at the modest kitchen, the signs of a life stretched too thin painfully evident. "I understand, Carol. I really do. But I have orders too. If I come back empty-handed again..." His voice trailed off, the unspoken consequences hanging heavily between them.

The room was suffused with a tense silence, broken only by the soft sobs of a cartoon on the TV in the next room. Carol's eyes were glassy as she nodded slowly. "I'll find something by this afternoon. Maybe I can borrow from…"

Her voice broke, the admission of her situation laying bare her vulnerability. Mike sighed, the business part of him at war with his humanity. "Okay, Carol. This afternoon. I'll come back then. But please, try to make it enough to show good faith."

As he stood to leave, Carol walked him to the

door, her posture weary but her resolve hardened. "Thank you, Mike. I'll have something."

Outside, Mike paused by his car, the heaviness of his role settling on him like the gray clouds overhead, threatening to break at any moment. He knew he'd be back later, and he dreaded what he might have to do.

CHAPTER TWO

Intersecting Lives

The cold dawn barely broke over the Detroit skyline, casting a pale light that seemed too weak to dispel the darkness lingering from the night. In a small, cramped kitchen, Carol stirred her coffee mechanically, her thoughts drifting back through the years like the steam rising from her cup. The walls of her home, filled with the echoes of her children's laughter and cries, seemed to close in around her, a silent testament to the journey that had brought her here.

Carol had once dreamed of more than this—of a college degree, a career, a home that felt more like a choice than a consequence. But life, as she had learned, seldom followed the path of dreams. The loss of her husband to a senseless accident had left her a single mother with two kids to raise and an avalanche of debt. Jobs had come and gone, each one promising a step forward but pushing her two steps back in a relentless dance of survival.

Across town, in an apartment that mirrored Carol's in its modesty but not its warmth, Mike sat at a similarly small table. His face was illuminated by the glow of his laptop, the numbers on the screen blurring into a mosaic of red and black. Once a small business owner, Mike had known the pride of self-sufficiency, his auto repair shop a local staple that served the community for over a decade. But the economic downturn that hit Detroit had spared few, and Mike was no exception. Debts mounted, credit lines snapped, and eventually, he found himself on the other side of those calls and knocks he now so dreaded delivering.

The screen flickered, a reminder of the precariousness of his current job as a debt collector —a job he had taken out of necessity, a daily compromise of his values. Each door he knocked on, each face that mirrored his own despair, chipped away at him. Yet, the irony of his work was not lost on him; he was but a cog in the machine that had once crushed him, now turning against others struggling just as he had.

As morning gave way to afternoon, Carol prepared for the inevitable. She sorted through old jewelry—a locket from her mother, a watch from her husband, items she had clung to through every previous storm. Each piece was a chapter of her life, reluctantly closed as she placed them in a small box.

Meanwhile, Mike's car rumbled to a start. His hands tightened on the steering wheel, each turn taking him closer to Carol's house, each mile a heavy tread back into the morass of his dual existence as both victim and agent of debt.

Their lives, disparate yet paralleled by struggle, were about to intersect once more. As Carol watched the street from behind frayed curtains, the sound of Mike's approaching car felt like the drumbeat of an encroaching fate. She opened the door with a resigned smile, the box of memories in her hand—a meager offering to the gods of debt.

"Mike," she began, her voice steadier than she felt, "I hope this can buy us some time."

Mike took the box, his eyes not meeting hers. "Thank you, Carol. I'll make sure this counts." His voice was low, each word weighed down by the heaviness of their shared plight.

As he drove away, Carol leaned against the doorframe, the empty box in her hands. The sky had darkened, clouds gathering as if in premonition. Inside, the silence was profound, a stark reminder of the cost of survival in a world that demanded far more than it returned.

CHAPTER THREE

Undercurrents

Carol's kitchen was dim in the early hours, the only light a flickering bulb that swung gently above the sink, casting long shadows across the linoleum floor. It was here, amid the quiet murmurs of a world not yet awake, that Carol sorted through what little she had left to sell. Each item she placed into the box was a relinquishment of a part of her past—a battered set of cookbooks, a collection of old vinyl records, and a few pieces of jewelry too modest to fetch more than a few dollars.

Her fingers paused over a small, wooden music box, a gift from her late husband on their fifth anniversary. She flipped open the lid, the delicate tune filling the room, stirring a swell of memories that she quickly stifled with a sharp intake of breath. "Can't afford to keep you," she whispered, tracing the intricate carvings before snapping it shut and placing it on top of the pile.

As the sun began to rise, casting a pale orange glow through the dusty window, Carol dragged tables to her front yard and set up her makeshift storefront. The items lay under the gaze of the early morning sun, each one tagged with a price that seemed both an insult to its sentimental value and a necessary concession to her dire needs.

"Morning, Carol," greeted Mrs. Henderson, her neighbor from two doors down, as she approached the yard sale. Her eyes were kind but pitying—a look Carol had come to dread.

"Morning, Linda," Carol replied, forcing a smile. "Looking for anything in particular?"

"Just browsing, dear. You know, supporting the cause," Mrs. Henderson murmured, picking up the music box. "This is lovely. How much?"

"Five dollars," Carol said, her voice steady despite the pang in her chest.

"Only five?" Mrs. Henderson clucked her tongue. "Seems like it's worth more."

"It probably is," Carol admitted, her eyes not meeting the other woman's. "But I need what I can get today, not tomorrow."

The morning wore on, and a few more neighbors and passersby drifted through, each sale a small victory and a larger defeat. Carol haggled when she could, but more often than not, she let items go for less than they were worth—each dollar a step toward staving off disaster, each transaction a piece of her history drifting away with strangers.

By noon, the crowd thinned, leaving Carol to sit back in a rickety folding chair, her eyes weary from the constant vigilance of the sale. Her stomach growled—the price of skipping breakfast to set up her yard sale. She considered making a sandwich but knew the bread needed to last through the week.

As she counted the day's meager earnings, Mike pulled up. His arrival was quiet, almost respectful, as if he understood the gravity of what he witnessed.

"Looks like you had some success," Mike said, stepping out of his car and nodding toward the tables.

"Some," Carol replied, standing to greet him. "Enough to cover half of what I owe. I'll find the rest somehow."

Mike looked around, his expression unreadable. "You're selling everything you own, Carol. There's got to be another way."

"And what would you suggest, Mike?" Carol's voice was sharp, edged with frustration. "I'm open to ideas because, from where I'm standing, options are about as thin as my next meal."

Mike sighed, his gaze falling on the small pile of cash in Carol's hand. "Let me talk to my boss again. Maybe there's something we can do—some kind of deferment or payment plan."

Carol nodded, her shoulders sagging slightly. "Thank you, Mike. I appreciate it, really. But I'm not just doing this for the rent. It's everything—utilities, school fees, food. It's like drowning in slow motion."

Mike's nod was heavy, burdened with the knowledge of her situation. "I'll see what I can do, Carol. Hang tight."

As he drove away, Carol turned back to her nearly empty tables. The music box was gone, along with pieces of her past she'd never get back. But her resolve hardened; this was not the end, not if she had anything to say about it. The fight was far from over, and Carol was no stranger to fighting.

CHAPTER FOUR

A Greater Force

The engine of Mike's aged Ford sputtered as he pulled away from Carol's curb, the rearview mirror framing her as she gathered the unsold remnants of her life. The weight of the day pressed heavily on his shoulders, a constant reminder of the battles fought on doorsteps like hers.

As he navigated the potholed streets of Detroit, his phone buzzed insistently from the passenger seat. Mike's jaw clenched; he knew without looking that it wasn't a call he wanted to take. At the next red light, he picked up the phone. The screen showed one missed message from Tony—a name that brought a swell of unease.

Gritting his teeth, Mike opened the message:

"Mike, we need to talk. Today. Don't make me look for you."

The words were stark against the glowing screen, each one a thinly veiled threat. Mike tapped out a response with shaking fingers, his usual composure slipping.

"Got it. I'll swing by."

The light turned green, casting a sickly hue through the windshield. As he drove, the city seemed to mirror his turmoil, with its graffitied walls and shuttered windows standing as monuments to desperation. Mike's mind raced, replaying every interaction with Tony, each one more strained than the last. Tony was not a man you wanted as an enemy, nor as a creditor. His methods were as ruthless as they were effective.

Mike pulled into a nondescript parking lot behind an equally unremarkable bar—the kind of place that thrived on anonymity. Tony was already there, leaning against a black SUV, his arms crossed, his expression unreadable. The setting sun cast long shadows, painting Tony in a sinister relief.

"Mike," Tony called out as Mike approached, his voice low and dangerous. "You're making me nervous, and I don't like to be nervous."

"Tony, I'm here, aren't I?" Mike retorted, his tone

more defensive than he intended.

Tony unfolded his arms, stepping closer. "You're late on your payments, Mike. This isn't charity. You know how this works."

Mike's gaze held steady, though his heart raced. "I know, Tony. I'm just trying to get things sorted. You'll get your money."

Tony smiled, though there was no humor in it. "I know I will. But here's the thing—you need to start making better decisions about who you collect from and how. You're too soft, Mike. Soft doesn't get the job done."

The threat hung between them, as palpable as the chill in the air. "I'm doing my best with what I've got," Mike replied, his voice steady despite the fear gnawing at his insides.

Tony stepped back, his eyes narrowing. "Your best better be good enough, or it'll be more than your job on the line. I suggest you remember that."

With a final piercing look, Tony turned and walked back to his SUV. Mike watched him leave, the threat echoing in his ears, mixing with the cacophony of city sounds that seemed suddenly ominous.

As he got back into his car, Mike felt the isolation of his position. The lines between right and wrong blurred under the harsh realities of his existence. His thoughts drifted back to Carol, to her resilience and her plight, and a spark of something fierce and defiant kindled within him.

With a renewed sense of purpose, Mike started the engine. He wasn't just collecting debts; he was surviving in a world that asked too much and gave back too little. And if Tony wanted a war, Mike would have to muster an army from the very people he sought to collect from—a united front of the broken, the brave, and the indebted.

The city stretched out before him, its shadows deepening, but Mike drove on, each mile a step toward an uncertain but inevitable confrontation.

CHAPTER FIVE

Tough Choices

The first light of dawn hadn't yet broken over the horizon, but Mike was already wide awake, the remnants of last night's confrontation with Tony lingering like a bad taste in his mouth. His home office was a shrine to better times — a framed article about the opening of his auto shop, photos of smiling customers beside cars they thought they'd never drive again. Now, those same walls felt like they were closing in, each memento a stark reminder of everything that had gone wrong.

His desk was buried under piles of overdue bills and final notices. The lamp cast a harsh light on the ledger in front of him, the red numbers far outnumbering the black. Mike ran a hand over his face, the stubble scratching his palm, a physical manifestation of the neglect he felt mirrored his life.

The phone rang, slicing through the oppressive

silence of the room. It was Lisa, his wife, calling from the hospital where she worked as a nurse and where their daughter, Emma, had been admitted days earlier due to complications from asthma. The weight of the ringtone was enough to make Mike's stomach churn.

"Hey, hon," Mike answered, trying to keep his voice steady.

"Mike, the doctor said Emma's responding to the treatments, but they want to keep her another night for observation," Lisa's voice was weary, every word soaked in exhaustion.

"That's good, right? She's getting better?" Mike clung to the hopeful part, desperate for any sliver of light.

"It is, but Mike... the insurance is giving us the runaround about the new medication. They're saying it's experimental and not fully covered." The frustration in Lisa's voice was palpable.

Mike's grip tightened on the phone. "I'll figure it out, Lisa. I'll talk to them and make sure they cover what they need to."

"I know you will," Lisa said, her faith in him a lifeline in the midst of chaos. "I just hate that it's come to this."

After hanging up, Mike sat back, his eyes scanning the room, landing on the small, crumpled flyer for a quick cash loan service. It was a desperate move, one fraught with risks and heavy interest rates, but desperation had become Mike's constant companion, whispering dangerous ideas that once would have been unthinkable.

He grabbed his coat and headed out, the early morning chill a slap against his resolve. The loan office was in a part of town that thrived on broken dreams and bad decisions. Inside, the air was thick with despair, the kind that clung to your clothes long after you left.

A man behind a reinforced glass window took Mike's application without a word, his eyes hollow, his movements robotic. Mike knew he was mortgaging his future, but the immediate need felt like a wild animal clawing at his insides.

"Application approved," the man said, sliding a check across the counter. "Remember, 30% interest, payments start next month."

"Thank you," Mike muttered, the words tasting like ash in his mouth as he took the check, each step out of that office heavier than the last.

Driving to the hospital, the check burning a hole in his pocket, Mike felt the enormity of his decision weigh down on him. He parked, took a deep breath, and walked into the hospital. The sterile smell of antiseptic hit him, a stark contrast to the griminess of the loan office.

In Emma's room, Lisa stood by her bed, her presence a calm in the storm. Emma was asleep, a peaceful expression on her face that belied the tumult of her recent days.

"We got the money, Lisa," Mike whispered, pulling his wife close. "She's going to be okay."

Lisa looked up at him, her eyes wet with relief and worry. "At what cost, Mike?"

Mike had no answer, his silence a heavy admission as he watched his daughter sleep, the tough choices he had made and the ones still looming large before him.

CHAPTER SIX

Harsh Realities

The city was cloaked in a deep twilight as Mike drove to the industrial outskirts where Tony operated his less-than-legal enterprises. A warehouse, seemingly abandoned, stood like a fortress against the encroaching darkness, its walls impenetrable and cold.

Mike parked his car in the shadow of an overpass, the rumble of the occasional passing truck vibrating through the chassis. He checked his reflection in the rearview mirror, straightened his collar, and exhaled a shaky breath. His heart thudded painfully against his ribs as he approached the warehouse door, the metallic clang of his knocks echoing ominously back at him.

The door swung open, revealing Tony's imposing figure, silhouetted against the stark fluorescent lights inside. "Mike, glad you could make it," Tony's voice was slick with mock warmth.

Inside, the warehouse was stark, the walls lined with shelves stocked haphazardly with items of dubious origin. Tony led Mike to a makeshift office in the corner, a desk littered with papers and a single lamp casting a harsh glow.

"Have a seat, Mike," Tony gestured to a metal chair. As Mike sat, Tony leaned against the desk, his face hardening. "Let's talk about your debt."

Mike swallowed, his mouth dry. "Tony, I've been pulling everything together. I just need a bit more time."

Tony scoffed, pacing slowly in front of the desk. "Time, Mike? Time is a luxury you don't have. You took money, promising returns. Where's my money, Mike?"

"I've got most of it," Mike stammered, pulling out an envelope stuffed with cash. "I just need another week for the rest."

Tony snatched the envelope, rifling through the contents with a sneer. "This isn't enough, Mike. You know how this works. You're short, and that makes me look bad."

Mike's voice was a blend of desperation and defiance. "I'm doing my best, Tony. I'm not trying to screw you over. I just need a bit more time."

Tony stopped pacing, standing ominously close to Mike. "Your best isn't good enough." He paused, his gaze cold and calculating. "You know, Mike, I hate doing this, but you're forcing my hand."

Tony snapped his fingers, and two burly men appeared from the shadows. The sight of them made Mike's stomach drop. "What's this, Tony?" Mike's voice cracked, his fear palpable.

"This is me ensuring I don't have to rely on your 'best' anymore." Tony's tone was chilling. "You have two days, Mike. Two days to get me everything you owe, or these gentlemen will be paying you another visit. Only next time, they won't be as polite."

Mike stood, his legs shaky. "You'll have it. I swear, Tony."

Tony merely nodded, his expression unreadable. "See that I do, Mike. See that I do."

As Mike walked back to his car, the night seemed darker, the weight of Tony's threats crushing him. The drive home was a blur, his mind reeling with the harsh realities of the world he'd become entangled in. The stakes were higher than ever, and now, it wasn't just his financial ruin on the line—it was his very life.

He arrived home to the quiet darkness of his house. Lisa was asleep, and Emma's soft breathing came steady and even from her room. The normalcy of the scene was a stark contrast to the violence of his evening. Mike sank to the kitchen floor, head in hands, as the gravity of his situation enveloped him. He was in too deep, and now, the safety of his family was tethered to his ability to navigate the brutal world of debt collection—a world where mercy was a weakness and every promise came with a threat.

CHAPTER SEVEN

Crossroads

The morning was overcast, gray clouds hanging low over the city as if mirroring Mike's turmoil. He drove to the meeting place, an old, abandoned lot on the fringes of Detroit, where rusted machinery and broken glass littered the ground. The air was thick with the stench of decay, the perfect backdrop for what was likely to be a contentious confrontation.

Tony was already there, leaning against the hood of his black SUV, a cigarette dangling from his lips. His presence dominated the bleak landscape, a predator in his natural habitat. As Mike approached, the gravel crunching under his shoes, Tony flicked the cigarette away, his eyes narrowing.

"Mike," Tony greeted him, his voice devoid of warmth.

"Tony," Mike replied, his voice steady despite the pounding of his heart. "We need to talk about the terms. There's got to be some way we can work this out."

Tony laughed, a harsh sound that echoed off the concrete ruins around them. "Work it out? Mike, you seem to forget your place. You owe me, and I set the terms."

Mike took a deep breath, trying to keep his composure. "Look, I can get you more money, but the timeline you're demanding—it's not feasible. I need more time."

Tony's expression darkened as he stepped closer to Mike, his stance aggressive. "You're in no position to negotiate terms, Mike. You fail to understand the gravity of your situation."

"I do understand, Tony. Believe me, I do," Mike insisted, his voice rising in desperation. "But pushing me like this—it's going to break everything. There won't be anything left to collect from."

Tony paused, considering Mike's plea, his face unreadable. After a moment, he spoke, his tone icy. "Alright, Mike. Here's what I'm willing to do." He took a few steps back, his arms folding over his chest. "I'll give you an extra week. That's it. But in return, I want a cut from anything else you bring in, not just your debt to me."

Mike's stomach churned at the proposal. It was a deal with the devil—more time, but at what cost? "And if I don't agree?" Mike asked, although he knew arguing with Tony was like arguing with a storm.

Tony's lips twisted into a smirk. "Then I guess you don't value your wellbeing—or your family's."

The threat hung in the air, heavy and menacing. Mike felt a cold sweat break out across his brow. "Okay," he said finally, the word like ash in his mouth. "One week. And you'll take the cut."

"Smart choice," Tony replied, his tone dripping with faux congeniality. "Don't let me down, Mike. You won't like the consequences."

As Tony drove away, leaving a cloud of dust in his wake, Mike stood alone amidst the desolation of the lot. The sense of entrapment was palpable, closing in around him like the walls of a cell. He knew he had just traded one form of bondage for another, more invasive and dangerous.

As he walked back to his car, the weight of his

decision bore down on him. He was out of options, driven to the edge by relentless demands. The path before him was fraught with moral and legal peril, but Tony's threat against his family left him no choice.

The drive back was a blur, his mind racing through possible solutions, each more desperate than the last. By the time he reached home, a plan began to form—a risky, last-ditch effort to break free from Tony's grip. It was a gamble, but Mike was out of moves.

He entered his house, the door closing softly behind him, sealing him in with his decision. Inside, he was met with the normalcy of his family's routine, a stark contrast to the chaos within him. He watched his daughter playing quietly, her innocence a painful reminder of what was at stake.

"Everything okay, Mike?" Lisa asked, looking up from her book, sensing the tension in his posture.

Mike forced a smile, the lie bitter on his tongue. "Yeah, everything's fine. Just another day." But as he spoke, the resolve hardened within him. He would protect his family, no matter the cost. The crossroads were behind him now, and there was only one way forward.

CHAPTER EIGHT

Echoes of Desperation

The sun had barely risen, casting a bleak, gray light over the city as Carol stood at her mailbox, her hands trembling as she extracted a slim, ominous-looking envelope. The final notice was stamped in bold, unforgiving letters across the front, and as she tore it open, the words inside confirmed her worst fears. Her landlord was losing patience, and eviction was imminent if she didn't settle her overdue rent within the week.

The kitchen was silent as she placed the notice on the table, the paper seeming to burn a hole through the wood with its severity. She leaned against the counter, her mind racing through her limited options, each more desperate than the last. The sound of her children getting ready for school was a distant murmur, a heartbreaking reminder of what she stood to lose.

31

Meanwhile, across town in a dimly lit garage, Mike stood before his old tool bench, now littered not with car parts but with plans and schemes, each more dangerous than the next. His hands were stained not with grease but with the ink of desperation as he pored over maps and timetables. The echo of Tony's threats reverberated in his mind, pushing him toward a dark precipice.

The garage door groaned as it opened, and Joe, an old friend and former employee, stepped inside. The look on Joe's face was grave as he approached Mike, his footsteps heavy with apprehension.

"Mike, are you sure about this?" Joe asked, glancing down at the plans spread out on the bench.

Mike wiped his hands on a rag, his gaze fixed on the papers. "It's the only way, Joe. I've run out of legal options. Tony's not the kind of man you disappoint."

Joe rubbed his neck, looking around the once thriving business now turned into a den of last resorts. "Breaking into the impound lot, stealing back cars that were towed for debts... Mike, this is serious time if we get caught."

"I know, Joe, I know it's risky. But if we can get these cars to the chop shop, sell off the parts... it might just be enough to get Tony off my back and keep my family safe."

Joe sighed, his expression torn between loyalty and fear. "And what about the fallout, Mike? What happens when people start looking for the missing cars?"

Mike's jaw clenched, his resolve hardening. "I've thought about that. We'll be careful, do it late, no one sees, no one knows."

Back in her home, Carol sat at the kitchen table, her fingers clasped tightly around a cup of coffee that had long since gone cold. The voices of her children drifted in from the other room, blissfully unaware of the storm gathering around them. She picked up her phone, her thumb hovering over Mike's contact. He had said once, if things got too tough, to call him. Perhaps there was something he could do, some way he hadn't thought of yet to help.

As she dialed, the ringtone sounded like a countdown, each tone a step closer to an unknown outcome. Mike answered, his voice low and weary.

"Carol, what's up? Is everything okay?"

"It's the rent, Mike. They're going to evict us if I

don't come up with the money by the end of the week. I... I didn't know who else to call."

Mike's heart sank, the weight of his own troubles compounded by the desperation in Carol's voice. "Okay, Carol, let me think about what I can do. Maybe there's a way to sort this out."

Hanging up, Mike stared at the plans on his bench. Now, it wasn't just about him or Tony; it was Carol and her kids too. His decision had just taken on a new layer of urgency.

"I'll figure something out, Carol. I promise," he whispered into the empty garage, his words an echo of desperation in the cold morning air.

CHAPTER NINE

The Breaking Point

The city's underbelly was rarely kind, and tonight it was particularly ruthless, the wind whipping through the empty streets carrying whispers of danger. Mike's heart pounded as he parked his battered pickup truck in the shadow of the impound lot's high fence, the barbed wire silhouette ghostly under the flickering street light. Beside him, Joe sat with his cap pulled down low, a silent testament to the gravity of their task.

"Are we really doing this, Mike?" Joe's voice was barely a whisper, his usual bravado nowhere to be found.

Mike glanced at his old friend, his own resolve firming. "It's the only way, Joe. We get in, get the cars, get out. Quick and clean."

They both exited the truck, their movements

synchronized, a result of years working side by side under the hoods of countless cars. Mike pulled out a pair of bolt cutters, the metal cold and heavy in his hands, as they approached the fence. A quick snip, and they were through, the world of legality and morality left behind with the discarded lock.

Inside, the lot was a graveyard of people's past mistakes and misfortunes—vehicles towed for debts or violations, each one a story of loss. They moved between the rows, their footsteps muffled, Mike's flashlight a beacon guiding them to their targets.

"Here," Mike whispered, stopping beside a row of cars marked for auction. "These three. Let's get to work."

The operation was mechanical, efficient. Within an hour, they had the cars hot-wired and ready. As they drove them out through the back exit, the thrill of the heist pulsed through Mike's veins, a dangerous mix of adrenaline and fear.

Meanwhile, across town, Carol sat in a brightly lit community center, her hands wrapped around a steaming cup of tea. The place was filled with the soft hum of conversations and the comforting scent of baked goods. She had come here on the advice of a neighbor, seeking assistance from a local support program aimed at helping residents avoid eviction.

A volunteer, a kindly woman with a reassuring smile, sat across from her. "Carol, I've reviewed your case, and I think we can help. We have funds available for emergency rent assistance. It's not a permanent solution, but it should give you some breathing room."

Carol's relief was palpable, her shoulders sagging as the weight of imminent eviction lifted slightly. "Thank you, I can't tell you what this means to me... to my kids."

"Of course," the volunteer replied warmly. "That's what we're here for. You'll need to attend a financial planning workshop as part of the agreement, and we'll need documentation of your employment and expenses, but I think we can get the check to your landlord by the end of the week."

As Carol left the center, a small spark of hope flickered within her, a stark contrast to the despair that had clung to her like a second skin. She texted Mike a quick update, a message of thanks and relief that cut through the darkness of his current undertaking.

Mike read the message as he parked the stolen cars in a nondescript warehouse on the outskirts of the city. The relief that Carol was safe, for now, was a balm to his frayed nerves. But as he and Joe wiped down the cars, erasing fingerprints and any trace of their presence, the reality of his choices settled around him like a shroud.

"We did it, Mike," Joe said, his voice low, a mix of relief and regret. "But at what cost?"

Mike didn't answer. He knew the cost was high, possibly higher than he had anticipated. As they left the warehouse, the early morning light beginning to edge over the horizon, Mike felt the weight of the breaking point not just on his shoulders, but deep in his soul, a fracture that he feared might never fully heal.

CHAPTER TEN

Darker Tides

The rain pounded relentlessly on the roof of Tony's sleek downtown office, the rivulets streaming down the windowpanes like tears on glass. Inside, the atmosphere was equally charged, the air thick with tension as Tony paced before a massive mahogany desk. Across from him, a man known only as Mr. Sorenson sat impassively, his cold gaze tracking Tony's every move.

"You've been falling short, Tony," Mr. Sorenson's voice was calm, but there was a lethal sharpness to it that cut through the ambient noise of the storm outside. "My employers are concerned about your... liquidity issues."

Tony stopped pacing, turning to face his creditor. His usual bravado was tempered by the gravity of the situation. "I understand, but the market's been tough. Collections are down across the board. It's not just me."

Mr. Sorenson tapped a finger on the armrest of his leather chair, a slow, deliberate sound that echoed ominously in the room. "Excuses are like debts, Tony. They tend to accumulate. What I'm interested in is solutions. How do you plan to address this shortfall?"

Tony leaned against the desk, his mind racing. "I'm expanding operations. Pushing harder on collections. I've even brought in some new guys who are... less conventional in their methods."

"Unconventional can be good," Mr. Sorenson mused, "as long as it produces results. My employers are not patient people, Tony. They expect their investments to yield returns, not excuses."

The conversation was interrupted by the buzz of Tony's phone. He glanced at the screen—a message from Mike indicating that a new, risky venture had just paid off. A flicker of relief passed through Tony's eyes, though he kept his expression neutral.

"I assure you, the money will be there," Tony said, a new confidence seeping into his tone. "I've got some irons in the fire that are about to pay off."

Mr. Sorenson stood, adjusting the cuff of his immaculate suit. "For your sake, I hope so. Because if not, we may need to reconsider our arrangement. And you wouldn't like the alternative."

As Mr. Sorenson left, the weight of the threat hung in the air, mingling with the smell of rain and leather. Tony sank into his chair, the relief from Mike's message short-lived as he considered the dangerous game he was playing. Not just with Mike and the little fish who owed him, but with the sharks who circled just beneath the surface of his operations.

Later that night, Tony stood on a rain-slicked street corner, watching from the shadows as his new enforcers worked over a late payer. The man's cries were muffled by the sound of the rain, his pleas lost in the cacophony of a city indifferent to his suffering.

Tony turned away, his expression unreadable. This was the world he had chosen, a world where debts were settled in pain and fear, and every dollar collected came soaked in desperation. He pulled out his phone, sending a curt message to Mike. "Keep pushing. It's working."

But as he slid the phone back into his pocket, the darkness of the night seemed to press closer, a reminder that in the world of debt, the tides were never in anyone's favor for long. The deeper layers of his network—the silent, watching creditors like Mr. Sorenson—were a constant reminder that his own position was as precarious as those he preyed upon. The storm above reflected the storm within, a turbulent reminder that no amount of rain could wash away the stains of his choices.

CHAPTER ELEVEN

Web of Threats

Lucia's penthouse overlooked the sprawling cityscape, her windows offering a view tinted with the glow of a thousand lives being lived below her level. The luxury was palpable, from the sleek, modern furniture that filled her expansive living room to the original artworks that hung on her walls, each piece a silent testament to her wealth. Yet, the opulence did little to mask the void that had grown within her, an emptiness that luxury could not fill.

She sipped her wine, a rare vintage that was more about status than flavor, and turned her gaze outward. The city lights blurred into a tapestry of anonymity, a stark contrast to the intimate, invasive nature of her business dealings in the debt trade.

The sound of her phone vibrating broke the silence, shattering her moment of forced tranquility.

It was Tony. Lucia answered with a click, her voice cool and controlled. "Tony, to what do I owe the pleasure?"

"Lucia, I've got good news," Tony's voice came through, tinged with a relief that he didn't bother hiding. "Cash flow's improving. We should be on track for this month's payment."

Lucia paused, letting the silence stretch between them for a moment longer than necessary. "That is good news, Tony, considering the alternative. I trust this means we'll have no further... inconveniences?"

"Absolutely," Tony assured her quickly. "You'll have what's yours."

She ended the call and stared at the screen, her expression unreadable. Lucia knew the world of debt well—a world where promises were as fragile as the lives they upended. She mused on the stark disparity between her life and those she drew profit from. Just that morning, her assistant had briefed her on various accounts, including a woman named Carol who was teetering on the brink of eviction—a situation all too common in her line of work.

As Lucia contemplated, her solitude was interrupted by a knock at the door. Her assistant, a sharply dressed young man named Andre, entered with his tablet in hand. "Lucia, there's a situation with one of the accounts—a property up for foreclosure. It's becoming a bit of a legal headache."

Lucia took the tablet, scrolling through the details with a detached precision. "Handle it, Andre. Use the usual methods. I want it resolved by the end of the week."

Andre nodded, hesitating as he added, "And the tenants? There's a family involved. Small children."

Lucia looked up, her gaze steely. "Compassion doesn't collect debts, Andre. Proceed."

As Andre left, Lucia turned back to the window, her reflection staring back at her—a visage of success that hid the ruthlessness required to maintain it. Down below, in the same city but worlds apart, Carol was likely preparing for another night of worry, her own reflection one of countless faces caught in the web Lucia wove so skillfully.

The juxtaposition wasn't lost on Lucia. She understood her role in the tapestry of the city's darker dealings, a thread woven through many lives, pulling some tighter and unraveling others. Yet, as she took another sip of her wine, the richness on her palate couldn't quite mask the bitter aftertaste of the realities she commanded.

Lucia's life, filled with the hollow trappings of wealth, was as bound by the web of threats she managed as were those who feared her calls. Each decision, each action, though wrapped in silk and velvet, was dictated by the ledger lines of profit and power, leaving her as much a prisoner of her empire as those who owed it their tears.

CHAPTER TWELVE

Thin Ice

Lucia's morning began not with the soft glow of sunrise filtering through her expansive windows, but with the harsh buzz of her encrypted phone vibrating against the cold, marble countertop of her kitchen. The screen lit up with a name that made her pulse quicken: Viktor. His calls were never good news—they were reminders that her empire was built on a foundation as stable as thin ice.

She answered with a neutral tone, her body tensed for the assault she knew was coming. "Viktor, to what do I owe the pleasure?"

"Lucia, let's dispense with the pleasantries," Viktor's voice was icy, his Russian accent thickening with his displeasure. "Your last payment was short. Again. This is becoming a habit, one I am not inclined to indulge."

Lucia inhaled slowly, her gaze fixed on the city below, as if the answer might be spelled out among the rooftops. "The market is tight, Viktor. Collections are up, but so are expenses. I'm not holding back anything from you."

"Then perhaps your methods are too soft," Viktor countered sharply. "You need to push harder. I will not accept another shortfall. Do you understand?"

She understood all too well. Viktor's threats were not idle; his reputation was built on decisive and often brutal actions. "I understand, Viktor. I will handle it personally."

The call ended, leaving Lucia with a silence that was anything but peaceful. She paced her living room, her thoughts racing. The empire she had meticulously built was more fragile than ever, and the pressure from Viktor was a weight she felt physically, a constriction around her chest.

As the day progressed, Lucia's usual composure was undercut by a simmering anxiety. She called in her team, her voice firm but laced with an undercurrent of urgency that was unusual for her. They gathered in her office, the tension palpable.

"We're tightening operations," she began, her eyes scanning the room, each member of her team reflecting a different shade of concern. "I want a twenty percent increase in collections by the end of the month. I will accept no excuses."

Her team nodded, the task daunting but clear. As they filed out, Lucia's assistant lingered. "Lucia, are you sure we can push that hard without legal blowback? Some of these accounts are sensitive."

Lucia turned, her face set. "Andre, ensure that the legal team is on their toes. I won't let Viktor down because of red tape. Make it happen."

The weight of leadership never felt heavier, and as the evening drew in, Lucia found herself alone in her office, the city lights twinkling mockingly at her distress. She poured herself a drink, the ice clinking hollowly against the glass—a stark reminder of her precarious position.

Her solitude was interrupted by an unexpected knock on the door. It was Andre, his face unusually grave. "Lucia, there's been a complication with one of the high-profile cases. It's escalated to a legal threat against us."

Lucia's hand tightened around her glass, the ice cracking under the pressure. "Handle it, Andre. Pay them off if necessary. I can't afford any distractions."

Andre nodded, understanding the severity of the situation. "I'll take care of it tonight."

As he left, Lucia stared out at the city, her reflection ghostly against the pane. The empire she fought so hard to uphold was on thin ice, the cracks spreading fast under Viktor's chilling influence. Tonight, she realized the full extent of her vulnerability—not just as a businesswoman but as a player in a game where the rules were dictated by those more ruthless than she.

The drink in her hand was no longer comforting, but a bitter reminder that in her world, warmth was a luxury she could not afford.

CHAPTER THIRTEEN

The Domino Effect

The city's relentless pulse throbbed under the cover of darkness, its arteries filled with the ceaseless flow of traffic and the distant sirens of an emergency that was always someone else's. In a less frequented part of town, where the gleam of streetlights failed to penetrate the alleys' deep shadows, a black SUV idled quietly. Inside, Lucia sat with her usual composed posture, her eyes cold as she surveyed the building across the street—a nondescript warehouse where Tony conducted his less official business.

Beside her, her most trusted enforcer, Marco, checked his weapon. The metallic clicks were oddly harmonious with the distant city sounds, a symphony of impending chaos. "We're ready on your go, Lucia," he murmured, his voice as taut as the grip on his gun.

Lucia didn't respond immediately, her mind replaying the conversation with Viktor. His threats were clear, and her options were dwindling. Tonight's action was a calculated risk, a necessary evil to shore up her faltering position. Finally, she gave a slight nod. "Do it. No fatalities unless absolutely necessary. I want Tony to remember who he's dealing with."

Marco nodded and stepped out of the vehicle, his figure melting into the darkness as he made his way towards the warehouse. Lucia remained, her expression unreadable, the faintest tremor of tension in her clasped hands the only betrayal of her inner turmoil.

Inside the warehouse, Tony was overseeing a late shipment of goods, unaware of the storm about to break over him. The laughter and casual banter of his crew filled the space, a stark contrast to the tension that coiled in the shadows.

The first sign of trouble was the abrupt silencing of the warehouse's side door alarm, a small but critical oversight in Tony's security. Within moments, the door burst open, and Marco's team poured in, their movements swift and practiced.

"What the hell?" Tony blurted, reaching for his own weapon, but he was too late. Marco had him in his sights.

"Tony, you should know better than to short Lucia," Marco said coolly, his gun steady in his hand. "Consider this a friendly reminder of your obligations."

The ensuing chaos was brief but intense. Tony's men, caught off guard, scrambled for cover, some attempting to return fire. Shouts, curses, and the sharp report of gunfire filled the air, the smell of gunpowder biting into the atmosphere.

Tony, held at gunpoint, could only grit his teeth as he watched his operation being dismantled with clinical efficiency. Marco's team was not there to kill; they were there to terrorize, to teach a lesson that Tony would not soon forget.

When the dust settled, several of Tony's men were down, injured but alive. The warehouse was a wreck, goods scattered, some destroyed. Marco approached Tony, pressing the cold muzzle of the gun briefly against his forehead—a final punctuation to the night's message.

"This is just a warning, Tony. Next time, we won't be as merciful," Marco whispered, then signaled his team to pull out.

Back in the SUV, Lucia received the confirmation of the operation's success. Her expression remained impassive, but her eyes reflected the weight of their actions. As they drove back towards the brighter parts of the city, the darkness seemed to cling to her, a reminder that each decision, each act of violence, pushed her further onto a path that was increasingly difficult to abandon.

The ripple effect of tonight's violence would reach far, touching lives beyond Tony's crew. Lucia understood this, the web of connections in her line of work too intricate to ever fully control. Each action was a domino, precipitating an endless chain of events, each more unpredictable than the last.

CHAPTER FOURTEEN

Spiral

The night was restless, with gusts of wind hurling leaves and trash against the grimy sidewalks of Detroit. Mike sat in his dimly lit living room, his mind spinning, unable to detach from the relentless churn of his thoughts. The heavy curtains blocked out the world, but not the cascade of consequences now knocking at his door.

His phone rang, the sound slicing through the silence like a warning shot. The screen showed an unfamiliar number, but instinct tightened his gut before he even answered. "Hello?"

"Mike, it's Tony." The voice was strained, carrying an edge of desperation Mike had never heard before.

"Tony? What's going on? Are you okay?"

"Far from it," Tony's laugh was hollow. "We had a visit from Lucia's goons tonight. They made a mess, sent a message. My operations are crippled, Mike. And that means our deal is in jeopardy."

Mike's grip tightened on the phone, his other hand balling into a fist. "What does that mean for us?"

"It means," Tony paused, the sound of a distant siren bleeding through, "it means the cash flow is choked. I can't cover my debts, Mike, and that means I can't cover what I owe up the chain, to Lucia, to her bosses... This isn't just bad for me. It's bad for you too."

The implication hung heavy between them. Mike's recent risky endeavor, the car thefts—it had been a desperate move to stabilize his standing with Tony, to prevent his own life from unraveling. Now, it seemed, he was standing on even thinner ice.

"Tony, listen to me," Mike's voice was urgent, "we can figure this out. There's got to be something we can do."

"The only thing you can do, Mike," Tony's voice was grim, "is prepare. Lucia's tightening the screws, and if I'm going under, it's going to splash over everyone connected to me. You need to brace yourself."

The call ended with a finality that left Mike feeling like he was gasping for air. He looked around his darkened home, the shadows seeming to close in around him. His family was asleep upstairs, blissfully unaware of the storm that was about to break over them.

Outside, the wind continued to howl, mirroring the chaos that now churned within him. Mike knew he had to act, to somehow shield his family from the fallout of Tony's disaster and Lucia's wrath. But the options seemed increasingly narrow, each path fraught with danger and moral compromise.

The next morning found Mike at his workshop, surrounded by the skeletal remains of cars he was supposed to be fixing, now potential collateral in a game far bigger than he'd ever imagined. His phone rang again, this time a number he recognized—Joe, his friend and unwitting accomplice in the recent car thefts.

"Mike, we got a problem," Joe's voice was tense, urgent. "The cars we lifted? They're hot, Mike. Hotter than we thought. There's heat coming from not just the local PD but from higher up. Someone's pushing this, hard."

Mike's heart sank further, a sinking stone in the pit of his stomach. "Keep your head down, Joe. I'll try to sort this out."

Hanging up, Mike leaned heavily against a workbench, his mind racing. The network of debts, threats, and now criminal activities was tightening around him, a noose that threatened to destroy everything he cared about. He needed a way out, a solution that could sever the ties that bound him to Tony, Lucia, and their dangerous world.

But as he stood alone among the remnants of engines and undercarriages, Mike felt the enormity of his isolation. The spiral of violence and debt was pulling him deeper, and for the first time, he wasn't sure if there was any way to claw his way back to the surface.

CHAPTER FIFTEEN

No Turning Back

Detroit's twilight cloaked the city in a blanket of oppressive heat and shadows as Tony paced the cracked concrete of his once-thriving warehouse. The damage from Lucia's enforcers was still visible —broken glass, charred remains of what used to be valuable goods. The air was thick with the smell of oil and desperation.

Under flickering fluorescent lights, Tony met with his remaining loyalists, his demeanor more volatile than ever. "We need to tighten our grip," he barked, his voice echoing off the bare walls. "Every single debtor, squeezed until they pay. I don't care what it takes."

One of his men, a burly figure with wary eyes, nodded. "What about the pushback? People are already on edge. We press harder, they might snap."

Tony slammed his fist against a metal table, the sound sharp and loud. "Then we break them. Anyone steps out of line, you make an example of them. No more Mr. Nice Guy. Got it?"

The group murmured their assent, unease palpable in the air. They dispersed, heading out into the night to enforce Tony's ruthless new directive.

Later that night, Mike received a furious call from Tony. "Mike, where's my damn money? You're dragging your feet while I'm out here bleeding!"

Mike's grip tightened on the phone, his patience fraying. "I told you, I'm working on it. I've got my own problems, Tony. The heat is on, from every direction."

Tony's voice was venomous. "Your problems are about to multiply if I don't get that payment. Remember, I know where you live, Mike. I know where your sweet little family sleeps."

The threat struck a nerve, igniting a fire in Mike. "You leave them out of this, Tony. I'll get you your money."

Hanging up, Mike was shaken, the threat against his family echoing in his mind like a death knell. His world was collapsing, the pressure from all sides becoming unbearable. He needed to collect outstanding debts, or face Tony's wrath—perhaps even protect his family from a very real danger.

The next day, Mike went to Carol's house, his demeanor dark, his mind racing with desperation. He knocked on her door, the sound more forceful than he intended.

Carol opened the door, her face weary. "Mike? What's wrong?"

"We need to talk about your debt," Mike said, his voice harsher than he meant. "It's past due. Way past due."

Carol recoiled slightly, taken aback by his tone. "I... I'm trying, Mike. I got some help from a community program, but—"

"I don't need excuses, Carol!" Mike interrupted, his voice raised, his own fears and frustrations boiling over. "I need money! Now!"

Carol's eyes filled with tears, her voice trembling. "I don't have it, Mike. I'm barely keeping my head above water."

Mike's gaze hardened, his heart pounding with a mix of anger and desperation. "Figure it out, Carol. Because if I go down, I'm taking everyone with me."

He stormed off, leaving Carol standing in the doorway, stunned and frightened. As he drove away, Mike's anger slowly dissolved into shame. He had crossed a line, driven by the violent undercurrents pulling him deeper into a world he despised.

Back at his dark, quiet home, Mike sat alone, the weight of his actions, Tony's threats, and the overall collapse of his moral world bearing down on him. He realized there was no turning back from the path he was on, yet he felt trapped, unable to see a way out that didn't lead to ruin. His encounter with Carol was a stark reminder of the man he was becoming—a man driven by fear, capable of threatening someone he once vowed to protect.

CHAPTER SIXTEEN

Collateral Damage

The tension in Detroit's air was palpable, a thick, choking fog that seemed to creep into every corner of the city. In the grim backdrop of a failing neighborhood, Carol's home stood, a beacon of her persistent struggle, the windows dimly lit as dusk fell. Inside, the sound of her children playing was a stark contrast to the growing storm outside her door.

Her phone rang, slicing through the laughter and light. It was Mike, and his voice was urgent, laced with a desperation that sent shivers down her spine.

"Carol, listen to me carefully," Mike said quickly, his words tumbling out. "Things are getting out of hand with Tony. He's lost it, and he's coming after anyone he thinks can cough up cash. You need to be careful."

Carol's heart pounded, her hand tightening on the phone. "Mike, what are you saying? What should I do?"

"Keep your head down. Maybe stay with a friend for a few days. Just... be safe, okay?"

After hanging up, Carol paced her small living room, her mind racing. The thought of fleeing her home brought a sharp pang of fear, but the danger was too real to ignore. She began to gather a few belongings, planning to take her children to her sister's house across town.

But before they could leave, the sound of heavy footsteps approached the door. Carol froze, her breath caught in her throat. There was a forceful knock, and a voice called out, "Open up! We know you're in there!"

Panicking, Carol peered through the window to see two of Tony's enforcers standing outside, their expressions grim and determined. Knowing confrontation would be futile, she opened the door, her stance defensive yet resigned.

"We need to talk about your debt," the larger enforcer, a man with a scar tracing down his cheek, stated flatly.

"I-I don't have anything to give," Carol stammered, her voice barely a whisper.

"Then we'll take what we can," the other replied, stepping past her into the house.

They began to rummage through her belongings, tossing aside her children's toys and books with careless brutality, grabbing valuables with rough hands. Carol watched, powerless, each of their movements a violation of the last vestiges of her security.

Her daughter cried, clinging to her leg, as her son hid behind the sofa, his small body trembling. "Please, just stop," Carol pleaded, her voice cracking. "You're scaring my children."

The men ignored her, continuing their ruthless search. They took her small TV, some electronics, and even the few pieces of jewelry she had managed to keep through her financial struggles.

As they left, one of them turned and sneered, "Consider this a warning. Next time, we'll not be so kind."

After they were gone, Carol slumped against the wall, her body shaking. The violation of her home, the terror in her children's eyes—it was too much to bear. She gathered her children close, trying to soothe them, her own tears mingling with theirs.

The night was long and full of shadows, each creak and whisper of the house a reminder of their vulnerability. Carol lay awake, staring at the ceiling, her mind a whirlwind of fear and despair. Mike's warning had been right, but the reality was harsher than she had imagined.

In the darkness, Carol made a decision. She would have to leave, to find somewhere safe where the shadows of debt and violence couldn't reach her family. The realization was heartbreaking, a resignation that her life, as she knew it, was being torn apart by forces far beyond her control. The collateral damage of debts unpaid was not just the items taken from her home, but the peace and security she had fought so hard to provide for her children.

CHAPTER SEVENTEEN

The Abyss

Under the harsh glare of a single flickering street lamp, Mike stood with his back pressed against the cold, rough brick of an abandoned building. His breath misted in the chill air, a visible testament to his anxiety. The deserted street felt like a stage set for a tragedy as the sound of an approaching engine broke the eerie silence. Headlights cut through the darkness, illuminating the cracked pavement and approaching doom.

The vehicle, a black sedan that exuded menace, came to a stop. The doors opened with a definitive thud, and Tony stepped out, flanked by two large figures whose sheer size was intended to intimidate. The dim light played off Tony's face, casting deep shadows that matched the darkening of his mood.

"Mike," Tony called out, his voice eerily calm against the backdrop of the silent night. "We need to talk."

Mike stepped forward, his hands empty and visibly shaking, showing he was unarmed and unthreatening. "Tony, I've been doing everything I can. I'm trying to gather—"

Tony raised a hand, stopping Mike mid-sentence. "You're trying, huh? Trying doesn't fill my pockets. You're running out of time and excuses."

One of Tony's associates stepped closer, a baton in his hand, twirling it with a menacing precision. The metallic sound it made sent a chill down Mike's spine. "Look, Tony, I need more time," Mike pleaded, his voice cracking under the strain.

"Time is a luxury you no longer have." Tony's voice was icy as he signaled his associate with a subtle nod.

The baton swung, landing a sharp blow on Mike's ribs. The pain was immediate and breathtaking. Mike doubled over, gasping for air, his body screaming in agony. "Tony, please," he gasped, the pain evident in his voice.

Tony stepped closer, his face inches from Mike's. "Listen to me very carefully. You have 48 hours to deliver the money, or next time we won't stop at just a warning. Your family, your friends—they're all fair game."

The threat hung heavy in the air, more terrifying than the physical pain. Mike nodded, desperation etching deep lines into his face. Tony turned on his heel and headed back to the sedan, his enforcers following, leaving Mike crumpled on the ground.

As the car's taillights disappeared into the night, Mike slowly pulled himself up against the brick wall. His mind raced through his dwindling options. He had stepped into a world of violence and threats he'd never imagined—far from the simple mechanic life he had once known. The abyss of criminal activity yawned wider, threatening to swallow him whole.

Limping home, each step was a battle against the pain and the overwhelming fear for his family's safety. The once familiar streets now seemed fraught with shadows and dangers lurking at every corner.

Arriving home, he found his wife, Lisa, waiting up for him, her expression etched with concern. "Mike, what happened? You look like hell."

Mike shook his head, a mix of pain and resolve in his eyes. "I've got to make things right, Lisa. I've got to protect us."

"What are you talking about, Mike? Protect us from what?"

He wrapped his arms around her, the fear and determination mingling in his embrace. "I've gotten us into a mess, but I promise, I'm going to get us out. No matter what it takes."

As they stood in their dimly lit living room, Mike knew he was standing on the edge of an abyss, facing choices that could either pull him from the brink or push him over. The stakes were life and death now, and he could no longer afford the luxury of hoping for a peaceful solution.

CHAPTER EIGHTEEN

Shattered Bonds

The atmosphere in Mike's home had shifted palpably, the air now thick with tension and unspoken fears. Lisa moved around the kitchen, her movements mechanical, her eyes avoiding Mike's. The intimacy that had once defined their relationship seemed like a distant memory, replaced by a chasm widened by secrets and danger.

Mike watched her from the doorway, his bruised ribs aching with each breath. He wanted to reach out, to bridge the gap with words of reassurance, but the right words eluded him. Instead, he broke the silence with a whisper of desperation. "Lisa, we need to talk about... about everything."

Lisa paused, setting down the dish she was drying. Her voice was tired, carrying a weight that seemed too heavy for her slender frame. "What's left to talk about, Mike? Every time you walk out

71

that door, I don't know if you're coming back. I don't even know who you are anymore."

Mike flinched as if her words were physical blows. "I'm still me, Lisa. I'm still the man you married, but things have... they've gotten complicated."

"Complicated?" Lisa's laugh was bitter, her eyes finally meeting his. "Is that what you call it when you're out there getting involved with criminals, when you're coming home with bruises and threats? That's not 'complicated,' Mike. That's a nightmare."

Across town, Carol faced her own crumbling reality. The recent intrusion by Tony's enforcers had left her shaken to her core, her trust in the neighborhood shattered. She packed boxes in silence, her children playing quietly, sensing their mother's distress but not understanding its depth.

Her phone rang, and she answered, hoping for a distraction. It was Mike. "Carol, how are you holding up?"

Carol's response was curt, a reflection of her strained state. "We're leaving, Mike. I can't stay here anymore, not after what happened. I can't trust that it won't happen again."

Mike's voice was heavy with guilt. "I'm sorry, Carol. I never wanted any of this to affect you."

"But it has, Mike. It has affected us," Carol replied sharply, her voice cracking. "I appreciate everything you've tried to do, but it's too much. I need to protect my kids, and I can't do that here."

Back at his house, Mike ended the call and looked at Lisa, who had been listening to his side of the conversation. "Everyone's getting hurt, Lisa. I can't seem to stop it."

Lisa approached him, her expression softening slightly. "Mike, you have to find a way out of this. Not just for Carol, not just for me, but for you. You're losing yourself in this... this war."

Mike nodded, feeling the truth of her words cut through the fog of his fear and desperation. "I know, I know I need to fix this. But I'm so deep in now, I... I don't know if I can."

The room fell silent again, the distance between them feeling more like miles than feet. Each was lost in their own thoughts, pondering the wreckage of their lives.

As night fell, the darkness seemed to seep into

the corners of their home, filling it with shadows that mirrored the ones creeping into their relationship. The bonds that had once held strong under the pressures of everyday life were now fraying, strained by the heavy burden of Mike's choices.

Lisa finally broke the silence, her voice a mere whisper. "Whatever you're planning to do, Mike, do it soon. We're running out of time."

Mike nodded, his resolve hardening. "I will. I'll make it right. Somehow." But as he spoke, doubt gnawed at him, the path forward obscured by the very darkness he was struggling to escape.

CHAPTER NINETEEN
End of the Line

The sky above Detroit was a tapestry of brooding clouds, the city beneath it a maze of tension and whispered threats. In the dimly lit backroom of his nearly deserted warehouse, Tony sat alone at an old, scarred table littered with unpaid bills and threats from his superiors. The weight of his crumbling empire pressed down on him, each decision leading only to further desperation.

His phone lay silent beside him, a stark reminder of his isolation. The recent brutal enforcement had only worsened his situation, pushing his debtors further away and deeper into hiding. He realized that his usual tactics were no longer working; they were desperate, not strategic. He needed a solution, one that would either salvage his standings or end his dealings for good.

The door creaked open, and his trusted

lieutenant, Marco, stepped in. The look on Marco's face was grim, mirroring the storm outside. "Tony, we've got another problem. Lucia's pushing for immediate payment. Says she's done waiting."

Tony rubbed his temples, feeling the onset of a headache that seemed to threaten his vision. "Marco, gather everyone. It's time we changed the game."

Within the hour, his crew, a mix of hardened enforcers and wary lieutenants, assembled in the warehouse. Tony stood before them, his presence commanding despite his evident fatigue. "Listen up," he began, his voice rough like gravel. "We've been on the defensive, reacting to every hit, every threat. No more."

He paused, letting his gaze sweep over the group. "We're taking the fight to them. We hit Lucia where it hurts. We disrupt her operations, her collections. We turn the tables."

A murmur of surprise and apprehension swept through the group. Marco stepped forward, a frown creasing his brow. "Tony, you sure about this? Going after Lucia isn't like hitting the streets. She's connected, powerful."

Tony's eyes narrowed, his decision firm. "I'm

aware. But think about it—she's as vulnerable as any of us. She relies on her reputation, her intimidation. We pull that rug out from under her, and she falls."

As plans were hastily drawn, the energy in the room shifted from fear to a grim kind of eagerness. They were used to fighting, but this was different. This was bigger.

Meanwhile, Mike received a frantic call from Tony, his voice strained but determined. "Mike, I need you on board with this. It's our only chance to break free from Lucia's grip."

Mike hesitated, his mind racing with the potential consequences. "Tony, this sounds like war. What about the fallout? What about our families?"

"There's always fallout, Mike," Tony replied sharply. "But we're already in the crosshairs. At least this way, we go out fighting."

Reluctantly, Mike agreed to join the risky endeavor, driven by his own desperation to protect his family and end the relentless pressure. "Alright, Tony. I'm in. But if we do this, we do it smart. No more reckless moves."

As the storm finally broke outside, unleashing

torrents of rain over the city, Tony and his crew prepared for a different kind of storm. Plans were made, routes mapped, and contingencies set. The air was thick with the electricity of impending action, a palpable tension that mirrored the thunderous weather.

Tony looked around at the assembled faces, their features set in determination. "This is it," he said quietly, almost to himself. "End of the line, one way or another."

The decision to confront Lucia head-on was a turning point, a pivotal move in the deadly chess game they were all a part of. For Tony, it was a final roll of the dice in a game where the stakes were life and death. For Mike, it was a desperate bid for freedom from the crushing weight of debts and threats. And for all involved, it was the moment that would define their fates, for better or worse.

CHAPTER TWENTY

Ties That Bind

The city was shrouded in darkness as the consequences of Tony's audacious move began to reverberate through the streets, echoing in the hurried footsteps of those caught in the crossfire. The once dormant threats had awakened, and now they prowled the night, leaving a trail of chaos in their wake.

In a nondescript safe house, Tony huddled with his closest confidants, their faces illuminated by the harsh light of a single bare bulb. Maps, photographs, and scribbled notes lay scattered across the table, each piece a fragment of their desperate strategy.

"We've stirred the hornet's nest, that's for sure," Marco remarked, his voice a low rumble in the tense silence. "Lucia's not going to take this lying down. Her reach is long, and her memory is longer."

Tony's eyes were steely as he responded, the weight of his decision pressing down on him. "It had to be done. We were sinking, Marco. At least now we have a fighting chance."

Across town in his dimly lit living room, Mike sat with Lisa, their hands clasped tightly together, a silent acknowledgment of the storm they were navigating. The phone call from Tony replayed in Mike's mind, each word a heavy stone in his stomach.

"Mike, are we going to make it through this?" Lisa's voice was barely above a whisper, her eyes searching his for an assurance he wasn't sure he could give.

"We have to," Mike replied, his voice firm despite the uncertainty that gnawed at him. "I made these choices, dragged us into this mess. I'll find a way out, for us, for our family."

At her modest apartment, Carol paced the floor, her children asleep in the next room, blissfully unaware of the tension that gripped their mother. She had spent the evening poring over legal documents and debt relief options, desperate for a way to sever the ties that bound her to this life of constant fear.

Her phone buzzed, a text from a number she didn't recognize. Hesitantly, she read the message, her heart skipping a beat as the words sank in. It was an offer from a community legal aid group, a potential lifeline thrown in her darkest hour.

Each character, ensnared in the web of their own making or by the designs of others, found themselves at a crossroads. The actions taken, the decisions made in desperation, now forced each of them to confront the reality of their situations and the need for a drastic change.

Back in his safe house, Tony looked around at his weary team. "We can't go back to the way things were," he stated, a new resolve hardening his features. "This fight with Lucia—it's just the beginning. We need a long-term plan, something that gets us out from under this life."

Marco nodded, his usual skepticism tempered by the gravity of their situation. "And if we can't find a way out?"

"Then we make one," Tony replied, his gaze unwavering. "We owe it to ourselves, and to everyone dragged down with us."

As the night deepened, the ties that bound them —whether of blood, debt, or duty—pulled tighter, a relentless reminder of the stakes involved. In the quiet moments between the chaos, each person faced the reality of their entanglements and the daunting task of disentangling themselves from a life they no longer controlled. The paths forward were fraught with peril, but the alternative was a descent further into the abyss, a journey none of them wanted to complete.

CHAPTER TWENTY-ONE
Reckoning

The city under the cloak of night was a different beast, its shadows deeper, its silences louder. Within the confines of an austere, dimly lit office, Lucia stood by the window, the cityscape sprawling beneath her like a chessboard of lights and shadows. She was a queen on this board, but now, her reign was under threat.

Her phone rang, shattering the silence with its ominous tone. She knew who it was before she answered—it was Viktor, and this call would determine her fate. With a steely resolve, she answered, "Viktor."

"Lucia, we need to conclude our business," Viktor's voice was cold, devoid of any emotion. "Your time to make good on your promises has expired. I am not a man of infinite patience."

Lucia's grip tightened on the phone. "I understand, Viktor. I'm aware of the stakes. I'm prepared to settle our accounts."

"Preparations are no longer sufficient. I want action, Lucia. If you fail to deliver, the consequences will be... severe."

As the call ended, Lucia felt the walls closing in. Viktor was not one to make idle threats. His influence was vast, his methods brutal. She needed a plan—not just to appease him but to ensure her survival in this cutthroat world.

Turning to her second in command, Andre, who had been waiting quietly by the door, she commanded, "Gather everyone. We need to accelerate our plans."

Within the hour, her team assembled in the conference room, a sense of urgency palpable in the air. Lucia laid out her strategy with precision. "Viktor is moving against us. We need to strike first. We'll redirect our resources, pull in favors, do whatever it takes. I will not go down without a fight."

Andre, ever the voice of reason, interjected, "Lucia, this could start a war. Are we ready for the fallout?"

"We have no choice," Lucia replied sharply. "It's either fight or succumb. I choose to fight."

The plan was radical—a series of calculated strikes against Viktor's operations, aimed at disrupting his cash flow and weakening his position. Each member of her team was assigned a role, their tasks critical to the success of the operation.

Meanwhile, across town in a nondescript building that served as Viktor's local headquarters, Viktor was receiving reports of unusual activities in Lucia's territories. His face remained impassive, but his eyes were like flint, sparking with the anticipation of the coming storm.

One of his lieutenants, a grizzled veteran of many such turf wars, leaned forward. "Boss, it looks like Lucia isn't going quietly. Should we increase our readiness?"

Viktor nodded, his decision immediate. "Prepare our enforcers. Increase surveillance on her movements. If Lucia wants a war, she'll get one. But make no mistake—we will be the ones to finish it."

As both camps prepared for the inevitable clash,

the city seemed to hold its breath, the tension like a bowstring pulled taut. Lucia, once a puppet master, now found herself a player on the board, her moves dictated by the desperate need to survive. Viktor, ever the strategist, was ready to exploit any weakness, his network of spies and soldiers at the ready.

The stage was set, the players poised, and as dawn crept over the horizon, the first moves were made, unseen yet profoundly felt. The city would soon awaken to a new reality, where the balance of power was either restored or irrevocably shifted. The reckoning was at hand, and no one involved would emerge unscathed.

CHAPTER TWENTY-TWO

Echoes of the Past

The city's muted lights cast long shadows across the room where Tony sat alone, whiskey in hand, staring at nothing. The silence was palpable, filled only by the distant sound of traffic and the low hum of the aging air conditioner. It was in this solitude that Tony's mind wandered back to the beginnings of his empire—a time that seemed both a lifetime ago and just yesterday.

Flashback: A Decade Earlier

The scene shifted to a younger Tony, full of ambition and ruthlessness, standing in the very same room, which was then bustling with energy and potential. "We're going to take this city," he had said to his small but loyal crew, his eyes alight with the fire of impending conquest. "Block by block, dollar by dollar."

Back then, the operations were small-time—loan sharking, minor gambling rings. It was a different kind of hustle, one that relied on street smarts and brute force rather than the complex web of influence and fear he would later weave.

Across town in a less affluent part of Detroit, a young Lucia was making her own moves. Ambitious and clever, she understood early on that information was power. Her network of informants grew, trading secrets for favors, laying the groundwork for what would become her vast empire.

Flashback: Lucia's Rise

In a dimly lit café, Lucia met with her first major informant, a disgruntled police officer with access to valuable data. "You keep me informed, and I'll make sure you're taken care of," she had promised, her voice smooth as silk but with an edge that hinted at the steel beneath.

These scenes from the past revealed the roots of their current crises. The debts began as mere numbers on a page, but over time, they grew, fed by ambition and greed, until they became the chains that bound them.

Flashback: Mike's Descent

A younger Mike appeared, vibrant and hopeful, opening his auto shop for the first time. "This is it, Lisa," he had beamed, his arm around his wife, who was pregnant with their first child. "A fresh start." But the economic downturn hit hard, and soon he was drowning in debt, each loan and favor a step deeper into the world he now struggled to escape.

The narrative returned to the present, the echoes of the past ringing loud in their minds. Tony swirled his whiskey, the ice clinking hollowly against the glass, a stark reminder of his cold, hardened path. Lucia sat in her office, her gaze fixed on the skyline, the lights below now symbols of her vast but vulnerable dominion.

As dawn approached, bringing with it the cold light of reality, these reflections on the past shaped their resolve for the future. Tony's eyes hardened with the memory of his rise—no one would take from him what he had fought so hard to build. Lucia adjusted the frame of an old photograph on her desk, a younger version of herself staring back; she would not be undone by the empire she had created.

Meanwhile, Mike, sitting in his darkened living room, looked at an old family photo, a stark contrast to the man he had become. His resolve solidified; he would do whatever it took to break the cycle, to reclaim the life he once envisioned for his family.

The past had set the stage, but the future was still theirs to write. As the city awakened, so did their determination to alter the courses of their intertwined destinies, each driven by the echoes of what once was, and what could still be.

CHAPTER TWENTY-THREE

Breaking Free

The dawn had barely touched the horizon of Detroit, painting the sky in shades of deep blue and gray. Carol stood in the sparse living room of her once cherished home, her bags packed at her feet, her children asleep in their rooms, oblivious to the pivotal change about to unfold in their lives.

Her hands trembled slightly as she dialed the number she had been given by a community advocate, a lifeline she had only recently discovered. The phone rang, cutting sharply through the silent anticipation of the early morning.

"Hello, Carol speaking. I need to speak with Ms. Hendricks, please," she said firmly when the line connected, her voice steadier than she felt.

"Speaking," came the reply, warm yet professional. "How can I assist you today, Carol?"

Carol took a deep breath, her decision weighing heavily on her heart but clear in her mind. "Ms. Hendricks, I've thought long and hard about this. I'm ready to move forward with the bankruptcy filing. I can't—no, I won't let this debt control my life any longer."

There was a brief pause on the line. "I understand, Carol. This is a big step, but it's a brave one. Filing for bankruptcy will give you a fresh start, free from these debts that have been holding you down. We'll need to meet and go over some paperwork, but I'll guide you through every step."

"Thank you," Carol replied, her relief palpable. "I want to protect my children's future, and if this is the way, then I'm ready to fight."

As she ended the call, Carol felt a surge of empowerment, a stark contrast to the helplessness that had plagued her for too long. She turned to her children's rooms, watching them sleep peacefully, unaware of the turmoil that had nearly upended their lives. In that moment, she vowed never to let the shadow of debt darken their doors again.

Later that day, Carol met with Ms. Hendricks at her office, a cozy yet efficient space lined with books on law and personal finance. They sat across from each other at a small table, documents spread out between them.

"As we proceed, remember that this is about reclaiming your life, Carol. It's not an end, but a new beginning," Ms. Hendricks advised, her eyes kind.

Carol nodded, signing each document with a sense of finality and liberation. Each signature was a strike against the cycle of debt that had tried to define her life.

Back in her neighborhood, as she loaded the last of her belongings into the car, her neighbor, Mr. Jenkins, approached her. "Heard you're moving out, Carol. Tough times?"

Carol smiled, a genuine expression of newfound hope. "Moving on, Mr. Jenkins. Starting fresh. It's what's best for me and the kids."

As she drove away from the life she once knew, Carol felt the weight of her past debts lift from her shoulders. She was breaking free, not just from financial chains, but from the fear and despair that had come with them. Her journey wasn't without its risks and challenges, but for the first time in a long time, the path ahead was hers to choose, a testament to her courage and determination to forge a better future for herself and her children.

CHAPTER TWENTY-FOUR
Downfall

The streets of Detroit, usually alive with the relentless hum of urban life, felt eerily subdued as the night drew in, a prelude to the storm that was about to erupt. Dark clouds hovered ominously above, mirroring the tension that gripped the heart of the city.

In a dimly lit warehouse on the edge of town, Tony and his crew prepared for what was coming. The air was thick with anticipation and the sharp scent of gun oil. Firearms were checked and rechecked, each click and snap echoing off the concrete walls.

"Tonight, it ends," Tony declared, his voice cutting through the murmured conversations. His eyes were hard, the lines on his face etched deeper by stress and sleepless nights. Around him, his men nodded, their expressions grim. They understood

95

the stakes—this was not just another skirmish in the ongoing turf wars; this was a fight for survival.

Meanwhile, Lucia, fortified in her high-rise office, overlooked the chessboard of lights below. Her security detail was doubled, each member acutely aware of the potential breach. Her phone rang, shattering the tense silence. It was Viktor.

"Lucia, you've played a dangerous game," Viktor's voice was cold, a verbal dagger. "You think you can undermine me and walk away?"

Lucia's response was measured, her voice betraying none of the adrenaline coursing through her veins. "Viktor, I've done what I had to do. I will not stand by and be a pawn in anyone's game—not even yours."

Back on the streets, Mike moved stealthily, his own mission clear but perilous. He had one chance to set things right, to extract himself and his family from the deadly web he'd become entangled in. His target was a critical data center housing financial records for Tony and Lucia's operations— information that could either incriminate them or exonerate him.

As he approached the building, the first drops of rain began to fall, the heavens opening with a fury that seemed to echo the chaos about to unfold. Mike picked the lock quickly and slipped inside, his heart pounding in his chest.

The data center was a labyrinth of servers and flashing lights. Mike located the main console, his fingers flying over the keyboard as he transferred files onto a drive. Every second was a gamble, every noise a potential alarm.

Suddenly, the sharp crack of gunfire erupted outside, snapping him back to the harsh reality. His time was up. Clutching the drive, he dashed towards the back exit, just as the door burst open in front of him.

In an abandoned lot, Tony's and Lucia's forces collided in a violent clash, the air filled with the roar of gunfire and the harsh cries of combat. Tony, amid the chaos, searched desperately for Lucia, his need for confrontation driving him through the melee.

Lucia, on the other side, armed and determined, advanced through the firefight. When she finally saw Tony, time seemed to slow. They raised their weapons, recognition flashing in their eyes.

"Lucia!" Tony shouted over the din, his gun aimed at her heart.

"Tony!" she responded, equally poised. "It doesn't have to end like this!"

But the cycle of violence, once set in motion, was relentless. Before another word could be exchanged, a stray bullet from the skirmish struck Tony, sending him staggering backward, his gun firing off into the darkness.

Lucia rushed to him, her anger dissolving into shock as she knelt by his side. Around them, the battle raged on, but in this small bubble of calm, the gravity of their actions came crashing down.

Mike, escaping just in time, heard the distant gunfire fade as he drove away, the data drive his passport to a new life. He looked back once, the city skyline a jagged line against the stormy horizon, a stark reminder of the world he was leaving behind.

As the dawn broke, washing the streets clean of the night's sins, the city bore the scars of its darkest night. Lives were changed, empires crumbled, and for those who survived, the future was a blank slate, tinged with the ash of their past.

CHAPTER TWENTY-FIVE

The Calm After

The dawn light filtered through the smog and debris of Detroit's streets, casting a pale glow on the aftermath of a night that had changed the course of many lives. The city, bruised and battered, was quiet, a stark contrast to the chaos and violence that had reigned just hours before.

In a small, nondescript apartment on the city's outskirts, Mike sat at a worn kitchen table, the data drive containing years of dangerous secrets lying next to an untouched cup of coffee. His hands were folded, his eyes haunted as he stared into the distance, grappling with the night's events and their irreversible impact on his life.

Lisa entered the room, her steps hesitant. The distance between them felt like miles. She sat down opposite him, her voice soft but carrying a weight of its own. "Mike... what happens now?"

Mike lifted his gaze, meeting her eyes. "I don't know, Lisa. I honestly don't. But whatever it is, we face it together. We're free of it, all of it. I made sure of that."

Lisa nodded, a mixture of relief and lingering fear evident in her expression. "And the others?"

"Tony's gone," Mike said quietly. "And Lucia... she's no longer a threat. It ended last night."

Across town, in a luxury high-rise now marred by bullet holes and shattered windows, Lucia sat in the ruins of her once pristine office. The empire she had built from the shadows was now exposed to the harsh light of day, its foundations shaken. Andre stood by her side, his loyalty unwavering despite the uncertainty of their future.

"We lost much, Lucia," Andre said, his voice steady despite the chaos around them. "Many will see this as a sign of weakness. We need to act quickly to recover."

Lucia turned to him, her demeanor still commanding despite her evident fatigue. "Rebuild," she stated firmly. "From the ashes, Andre. We will rebuild. But differently this time. We have to be smarter, not just stronger."

Meanwhile, Carol, having moved to a small town some miles away, watched her children play in the yard of their new home, a modest but safe haven from the storms of their past. The fear and uncertainty that had once clouded her days were now replaced by a cautious optimism. She had a new job, a new community, and most importantly, a new start.

As she hung laundry on the line, her neighbor, an elderly lady named Mrs. Wilkins, called out, "Settling in well, Carol?"

Carol smiled, the sun warm on her face. "Yes, thank you. It feels good to start over."

Back in the city, the consequences of the previous night's events continued to ripple through the streets. News reports buzzed with the downfall of a local crime lord and the mysterious circumstances surrounding the violent clashes in the industrial district.

In his apartment, Mike turned off the television, unwilling to relive the events through the media's lens. He looked at Lisa, taking her hand. "It's over, Lisa. Whatever comes next, we're free from the past."

Lisa squeezed his hand back, a silent acknowledgment of their new reality. They had survived, but survival came at a cost. Now, they needed to rebuild, to forge a new path forward from the remnants of their old lives.

As the city began to wake, the calm after the storm settled in, a quiet reminder that even in the darkest times, the sun would rise, offering a new day and new beginnings.

CHAPTER TWENTY-SIX

New Beginnings

The early morning light cast a soft glow over the city, illuminating the streets that had witnessed chaos just days before. Now, there was a deceptive peace, a calm that belied the underlying tensions still simmering among those left to pick up the pieces.

In a modest community center, Carol sat across from a counselor, a middle-aged woman named Janet who specialized in trauma and recovery. They were surrounded by serene blue walls and motivational posters, a stark contrast to the turmoil Carol had experienced.

"I feel like I'm finally breathing again," Carol confessed, her hands wrapped around a cup of steaming tea. "But at night, I still hear the sounds of that night. The breaking, the shouting..."

"It's normal to feel that way after what you've been through," Janet responded gently. "Recovery is a journey, Carol. It doesn't end with moving to a new place or escaping a situation. It's about healing the wounds that aren't visible."

Carol nodded, taking in the truth of Janet's words. "I want to heal, not just for me, but for my kids. They deserve a mother who is present, not lost in her fears."

"Focus on building new routines, new memories. It's a powerful way to reclaim your narrative," Janet advised, offering a compassionate smile.

Across town, Mike and Lisa were in the midst of their own new beginning. They had just signed the lease on a small garage Mike planned to turn into a mechanic shop, hopeful to revive his old career in a way that aligned with his renewed values.

"This is it, huh?" Lisa remarked, looking around the still-empty space that would soon be buzzing with activity.

"It's a start," Mike replied, his voice tinged with cautious optimism. He walked over to the large front window, wiping a smudge from the glass. "A clean slate, Lisa. No more shortcuts, no more looking over our shoulders."

Lisa joined him by the window, her hand finding his. "Just us, doing it the right way this time."

Meanwhile, Lucia was dealing with the remnants of her crumbled empire. Her luxurious apartment now felt like a gilded cage, each opulent decoration a reminder of what she had lost. With Andre at her side, she was planning her next steps, not to rebuild her empire, but to dismantle what was left in a controlled manner.

"We need to ensure that our exit from the game doesn't leave a vacuum that could cause more chaos," Lucia explained, her eyes scanning multiple digital screens displaying various assets and accounts.

Andre, ever the loyal lieutenant, nodded in agreement. "I'll make sure everything is handled discreetly. And what about you, Lucia?"

Lucia paused, her gaze turning toward the city skyline. "I'm leaving Detroit. It's time for a change, maybe a chance to find a semblance of the peace I sacrificed a long time ago."

Each character, in their own way, was taking steps on new paths forged by the trials they had endured. The city, too, seemed to be in a phase of rebuilding, the community coming together to heal and to bolster the fragile peace that had settled in the wake of the storm.

As the chapter closed on their past lives, the dawn of new beginnings promised a future where the lessons learned from pain and loss paved the way for growth and redemption. Each step forward was marked not by the echoes of past misdeeds but by the quiet strength of hope and the determination to do better.

CHAPTER TWENTY-SEVEN

Reflections

As the city of Detroit bathed in the soft light of a late afternoon, each character found a moment of solitude to reflect on the tumultuous paths that had led them here, each contemplating the profound lessons carved into their lives by recent events.

Mike stood in the center of his new mechanic shop, tools neatly arranged, everything in its place —a stark contrast to the chaos of his former life entangled in debts and threats. The quiet of the shop gave him space to think, the smell of oil and metal grounding him in his new reality.

He leaned against a freshly painted workbench, speaking softly to himself, "All those years chasing easy money, thinking I was doing it for the family. But what they really needed was me, present and not lost in schemes." He paused, his gaze sweeping over the shop. "This time it's different. This time, I

107

build something lasting, something clean."

Carol sat on the porch of her new home, watching her children play in the fading light. The quiet of the suburban street was a gentle balm after the harshness of their previous life. She held a journal, a habit she had taken up to process her experiences and solidify her resolve.

Writing in her journal, she noted, "Moving was the hardest decision, filled with fear of the unknown. But it taught me that sometimes, the hardest choices are the most necessary. I learned that resilience isn't just enduring but knowing when to leave, to step towards a better future for me and the kids."

Lucia stood at the window of her once opulent office, now stripped of its luxuries, a symbolic gesture of her shift from power broker to someone seeking redemption. She turned to Andre, who had remained by her side, her tone reflective.

"Do you ever think about how it all started, Andre? We thought we were climbing to the top, but we were actually digging ourselves deeper into a hole." She shook her head slightly. "I've learned that power built on fear is fleeting. It's time to find strength in honesty, even if it means starting from scratch."

Though Tony had met a tragic end, his legacy lived on in the memories of those he had influenced. In a quiet, dimly lit room, his brother, who had quietly watched Tony's rise and fall, sat contemplating a photo of the two of them, younger, full of hope and naivety.

Speaking to the memory of his brother, he murmured, "You chased the shadows thinking they led to glory, but they only led to darkness. I learned through you that ambition without conscience is a perilous path. I hope wherever you are now, you find the peace that eluded you in life."

As the day waned, each character continued their contemplation, understanding more deeply the costs of their choices and the value of the lessons learned. Detroit, the city that had both cradled and crushed their dreams, stood silently around them, a testament to resilience and renewal.

This moment of reflection marked not an end but a beginning, a preparation for the chapters of life yet to be written, informed by the hard-earned wisdom of their pasts. In the quiet aftermath of their turmoil, they found not just regrets but a renewed sense of purpose, each in their own way ready to face the future with a clearer vision and a stronger spirit.

CHAPTER TWENTY-EIGHT

The Final Bet

The vibrant neon lights of the casino flashed in mesmerizing patterns, casting colorful reflections on the polished floors. The cacophony of slot machines, the clatter of roulette balls, and the soft rustle of cards blended into a symphony of temptation and risk. Tonight, the casino had attracted its usual array of hopefuls, but none as poised for the gamble as Viktor.

Viktor strode through the casino with the air of a man who owned the world—or at least believed he did. Dressed in a sharply tailored suit, his presence commanded attention, and his eyes, cold and calculating, missed nothing. He approached the high-stakes roulette table, a smirk playing on his lips.

"Evening," he greeted the croupier, his voice smooth and confident. "I believe fortune favors the bold tonight."

The croupier nodded, accustomed to the bravado of high rollers. "Welcome, sir. Will you be playing the usual?"

Viktor nodded, placing a briefcase on the table. He opened it, revealing stacks of bills, a visual testament to his recent victories and unshaken confidence. "All on black," he declared, his tone leaving no room for doubt.

A murmur rippled through the surrounding crowd. Such bets were not uncommon in this place, but the audacity to wager such a sum in a single bet was both admired and admonished.

The croupier nodded, setting the wheel in motion with practiced ease. The ball clattered across the spinning wheel, the sound a heartbeat in the suspense-filled atmosphere.

Viktor watched, his expression unreadable. Around him, spectators held their breath, drawn into the drama of the gamble. The wheel began to slow, the anticipation building to a crescendo until the ball landed with a definitive clink.

Red.

A collective gasp escaped the crowd. Viktor's expression hardened, the initial shock quickly giving way to a stoic acceptance. He had lost— everything. The finality of it settled over him, a rare moment of vulnerability flashing across his face before he regained his composure.

"Well played," he said to the croupier, his voice devoid of the confidence that had filled it just moments before. He closed his briefcase, now significantly lighter, and turned to leave.

As he walked away, his mind replayed the gamble, the loss, and the broader implications. This loss was not just about money; it was a symbolic defeat, a crack in the armor of a man who had thought himself invincible.

Outside, the night air was cool against his heated skin, a stark contrast to the stifling atmosphere of the casino. Viktor paused, looking back at the flashing lights. He realized that his hubris had not only cost him financially but had also exposed a crucial weakness in his character.

"Perhaps," he mused aloud, "there's more to learn from defeat than from victory."

As Viktor disappeared into the night, the casino resumed its usual pace, the roulette wheel spinning again, ready for the next hopeful gambler. In the world of high stakes, fortunes were made and lost every night, but for Viktor, the true gamble had been one of self-discovery, a bet that would define his next moves in the game of life.

CHAPTER TWENTY-NINE
Black and Red

The casino's opulent main floor was alive with the sounds of fortune and despair, the clinking of chips and the soft murmur of spectators blending into a symphony of chance. Viktor, once a titan among men, now reduced to a mere participant in the gamble, stood once more before the roulette table, his entire demeanor one of grim determination.

With the last of his cash reserves at stake, he placed his chips on black, a silent prayer escaping his lips—a prayer to the gods of chance and fate, who seemed to have abandoned him as of late. The croupier nodded, his professional detachment a stark contrast to the tense lines of Viktor's face.

"Final bets," announced the croupier as he spun the wheel with a practiced flick. The room seemed to hold its breath, the air thick with anticipation.

Viktor watched, his heart pounding, as the ball danced around the spinning wheel. It clattered with mocking indecision before finally settling. Red.

A hush fell over the crowd. Viktor's face drained of color, his stance deflated in defeat. The weight of the loss was more than financial—it was existential. His fortune, amassed over a lifetime of ruthlessness and strategic calculation, had evaporated into the casino's charged atmosphere.

The croupier cleared his throat, breaking the palpable silence. "I'm sorry, sir."

Viktor waved him off, a bitter smile twisting his lips. "No, you're not. Why would you be?" He turned from the table, his steps heavy as he navigated through the maze of tables and slot machines, each step echoing the finality of his downfall.

Outside, the neon lights of the casino buzzed and flickered, a garish mockery of his failure. He paused, lighting a cigarette, the smoke curling up into the dark sky, mingling with the chilly night air.

"You played the game, Viktor," he muttered to himself, the smoke stinging his eyes—or perhaps that was something else, a rare show of vulnerability. "And you lost. Not just money, but everything."

The realization hit him fully then, the enormity of his gamble with life and morality. He had lived on borrowed time, with borrowed money, always pushing the limits, thinking he was controlling the game. Tonight, the roulette wheel had taught him otherwise. Life, he understood now, was not a game to be controlled, but a journey to be experienced, with all its chaos and unpredictability.

As he tossed his cigarette and watched it extinguish on the wet pavement, Viktor made a decision. It was time to leave this life behind. Perhaps somewhere new, somewhere far from the world of debts and deceit, he could find a semblance of peace. Maybe there, he could rebuild, not his fortune, but himself.

The story concludes with Viktor walking away from the bright lights of the casino, his silhouette gradually disappearing into the night. The roulette wheel continued to spin behind him, indifferent to his departure, ready for the next gambler to challenge fate. The final image is one of the roulette wheel, still spinning, a stark reminder of the perpetual motion of life and chance, where every spin might bring a new beginning or another downfall.

Made in the USA
Columbia, SC
29 July 2024